Garrison Keillor

THE OLD MAN WHO LOVED CHEESE

Illustrated by
Anne Wilsdorf

ff

faber and faber

To Malene, who does not care for cheese at all
G. K.

To Berivan, my sweet and
tasty little fresh-goat-cheese-like daughter
A. W.

First published in the USA and Canada in 1996 by Little, Brown and Company

First published in Great Britain in 1996
by Faber and Faber Limited
3 Queen Square London WC1N 3AU

Printed in Hong Kong

Text © Garrison Keillor, 1996
Illustrations © Anne Wilsdorf, 1996

Garrison Keillor is hereby identified as author of this work in accordance with
Section 77 of the Copyright, Designs and Patents Act 1988

A CIP record for this book is available from the British Library

ISBN 0–571–17902–9

There was an old man named Wallace P. Flynn
Who lived in a house in the trees —
You could smell him for several miles downwind
Because of his fondness for cheese.

For the cheese that was dear to W.P.
Was not the mild kind, such as Brie,
The cheese of polite society —
No, he liked cheese that was *in your face!*
That smelled like socks from a marathon race,
Cheese that really stank up the place!

His wife knelt down and begged him, "Please,
Have mercy, Wallace, and change your cheese!"

His son said, "Cheese makes your breath so bad,
It smells like death to be near you, Dad!"

His daughter asked him, "What is the sense of
Eating cheese that is so *offensive?*"

Said Wallace P., "It's offensive to you
But *cheese cheers me up* when I am blue.
I don't know why, but a nice sharp cheddar
Makes me feel a whole lot better!
A Limburger or Emmentaler
Makes me grin and jump and holler!
And oh, the pleasure!
Of a slice of Cheshire!
Some men want fame and their name on marquees.
Some men love money. *I choose cheese.*"

So his daughter moved to Oklahoma
To escape the aroma;

And his son ran off to Arkansas,
Which has a Halitosis Law;

And his wife, Louise,
Sailed away to the Hebrides
Islands, where an ocean breeze
Steadily blows by night and day
And drives unpleasant smells away.

With his family gone, Wallace P. Flynn
Lost all of his self-discipline.
He ate cheese morning and night,
Cheese so strong that his hair turned white.

He walked around with a cheesy grin.
He'd drive his truck to town and park it
In front of Easy Ed's Used Cheese Market.

Easy Ed was a skinny old geezer,
With little green eyes and a great big beezer,
Who sold old cheese that he stored in rooms
Deep underground in cool, dark tombs,
Cheese that was covered with thick green mold.
Some of the cheese was twenty years old!

Wallace P. Flynn drove his load of cheese
Back to his lonely house in the trees—
To him, it smelled like fresh spring blooms,
Sweet and pure and good and rich—
While other drivers swerved into the ditch,
Overcome by deadly fumes.

He wrapped the cheese in a burlap sack
And buried it deep in a hole out back
And covered it up and put in a pipe,
So he could smell when the cheese got ripe.

And when it began to gurgle and squish
And bubble and burble and smell like dead fish,

He heard the gurgles and bubbles and squishes
And cried, "By George! It smells delicious!"

The smell was so awful, so sour and vile,
The skunks had to go and lie down for a while.

The squirrels picked up all the nuts they had squirreled
And moved to a distant part of the world.

One day, a pig stood up on its haunches
And fell over flat on its back, unconscious.

The smell became so fetid and rank,
The mailman bought an oxygen tank.
Good heavens, how the neighborhood stank!

There were stories in the papers
About the terrible vapors:
"Despite Neighbors' Pleas,
Flynn Still Chomps Cheese."

The neighbors called the cheese police,
Who ordered Wallace P. Flynn to *Cease!*
"We're coming in! Throw down your cheese,
And put your hands in the air and freeze!"
They cried, advancing through the trees.

They wore cheeseproof masks and cheeseproof suits
And rubberized steel-toed anticheese boots,
More expensive than a pair of Guccis
And strong enough to keep out blue cheese.

But Wallace P. Flynn locked his door,
And sat on the floor and ate some more
Norwegian cheese, which he dug up and which
He spread on bread and made a sandwich.

Green putrid cheese — oh, how it stunk!
Glops and blobs and drops and drips —
From yellow lumps of rotten gunk
That oozed through his teeth and between his lips.

The cheese police surrounded the place,
But tears ran down the captain's face —
He grabbed a tree and stood quite still —
The smell had made him rather ill —

His face was pale, his knees were weak,
Strong tremors shook his great physique,
He gasped for breath, his eyes went dim,
That cheese was much too strong for him.

"Halt!" he cried, and then, "Retreat!"
And gave his men a backward nod,
And they turned and ran back to the street,
The Cheese Brigade of the Diet Squad,
And stood in rather loose formation,
Engaged in rapid respiration.

The captain did not stand there, flustered,
But ordered the men to load their guns
With butterscotch custard and sticky buns.
They fired once, and again —*Bang! Bang!*—
And then a blast of lemon meringue —

And out of the house came a pitiful cry:
"Stop the custard! Please! No more!
The smell of lemon makes me gag!"
And Old Man Flynn came out the door
With his hands held high,
Holding a big white flag.

They took him away, the poor old man,
And drove to town in a caravan,

And eventually the case was tried
In court by chief judge Jacqueline Hyde,
And a jury sat there bleary-eyed
As hundreds of experts testified;

And they talked and talked and couldn't decide,
And Halloween came, and Christmastide —
When Wallace Flynn Jr. stood up and shouted,
"Give up cheese, Daddy! Do without it!"

He had just flown in from Arkansas
With his wife, Eloise, and his mother-in-law
And a baby boy, Wallace Flynn the Third.

"Look," he said, "you've become a grandpa!
If you love your family, give your word—
From this day on,
No Parmesan!
Promise you won't eat a
Bite of Velveeta.
Swiss, Romano, Roquefort, Edam—
Give 'em up, Daddy, you don't need 'em!
Why devote your life to cheese
When you can have a grandbaby on your knees?"

Wallace P. Flynn looked at Wallace No. 3,
And the child smiled so beautifully
And held out his tiny hands so wide,
The old cheesehead broke down and cried.

"I do relinquish and forswear
All cheese, including Camembert,
Colby—and even my Monterey Jack
Gift pack
From my aunts in
Wisconsin.
I never again will face a
Schmierkase.

From now on, this shall be my goal: a
Life of zero Gorgonzola.
No cheese and macaroni or cheese on my beans;
I am all done with cheese cuisines.
Tuna melts and potatoes au gratin
Shall be (by me) henceforth forgotten."

And the judge said, "Mr. Flynn, your *No Cheese* pledge is all we need. Now go. You're free." And the jury whooped and cried, And his daughter ran to the old man's side And kissed his cheek and stroked his hair And whispered, "Daddy, we love you so," And his son wore a smile a mile wide And he tossed the baby in the air And the baby laughed—it was quite the show!

Wallace P. Flynn took the whole Flynn bunch
Around to a corner cafe for lunch.

He enjoyed a plate of garden peas,
A Chinese salad with anchovies,
Fresh fruit flown in from overseas,
Cherries and berries and jujubes,
And two iced teas.

The waitress looked at W.P.
"Is there anything else you'd like?" said she.
"No thanks," he said. "This is all for me.
All I want is my family."

That night, he sailed to the Hebrides,
Back to the arms of his dear Louise,
And they bought a cottage in a grove of trees,
Where humbly buzzed the bumblebees
Among the petunias and peonies.

And Mr. and Mrs. Wallace P. Flynn
Felt right at home by the oceanside,
Watched the tide go out and the tide roll in,
And were very deeply satisfied,
With sunny days and beautiful views,
A low-fat lunch and a daily snooze,

Which goes to show that a person can choose
To mend his ways and to begin
A brand-new life,
As Mr. Flynn did with his wife.